Mark Sperring

Laura Ellen Anderson

SNAPPY BIRTHDAY

BLOOMSBURY

LONDON   NEW DELHI   NEW YORK   SYDNEY

One day an invitation
came to number 24.
It was from a next door neighbour
who they'd never met before.
It said . . .

COME TO MY
BIRTHDAY PARTY
(it's at number 22).

I really, really, really
want to celebrate with you!

So PLEASE just bring your
little selves
(don't bring a thing for me).

The NICEST gift of ALL would be

TO HAVE YOU ALL
FOR
TEA.

There wasn't much to think about –
of course they had to go.
For, who doesn't like a party?
Well . . . nobody I know!

So, they ran up to their bedrooms
and pulled out things to wear,

with stripes and spots
and lots of dots
and ribbons everywhere!

And while they all got ready,
they chatted merrily
about the treats that lay in store
and who their host could be . . .

Yes, who had sent that invite?
And what would they be like?
It must be someone lovely!
(But – hmm – would they be right?)

When they arrived that afternoon
at number 22,
the front door swung right open
and a voice cried out . . .

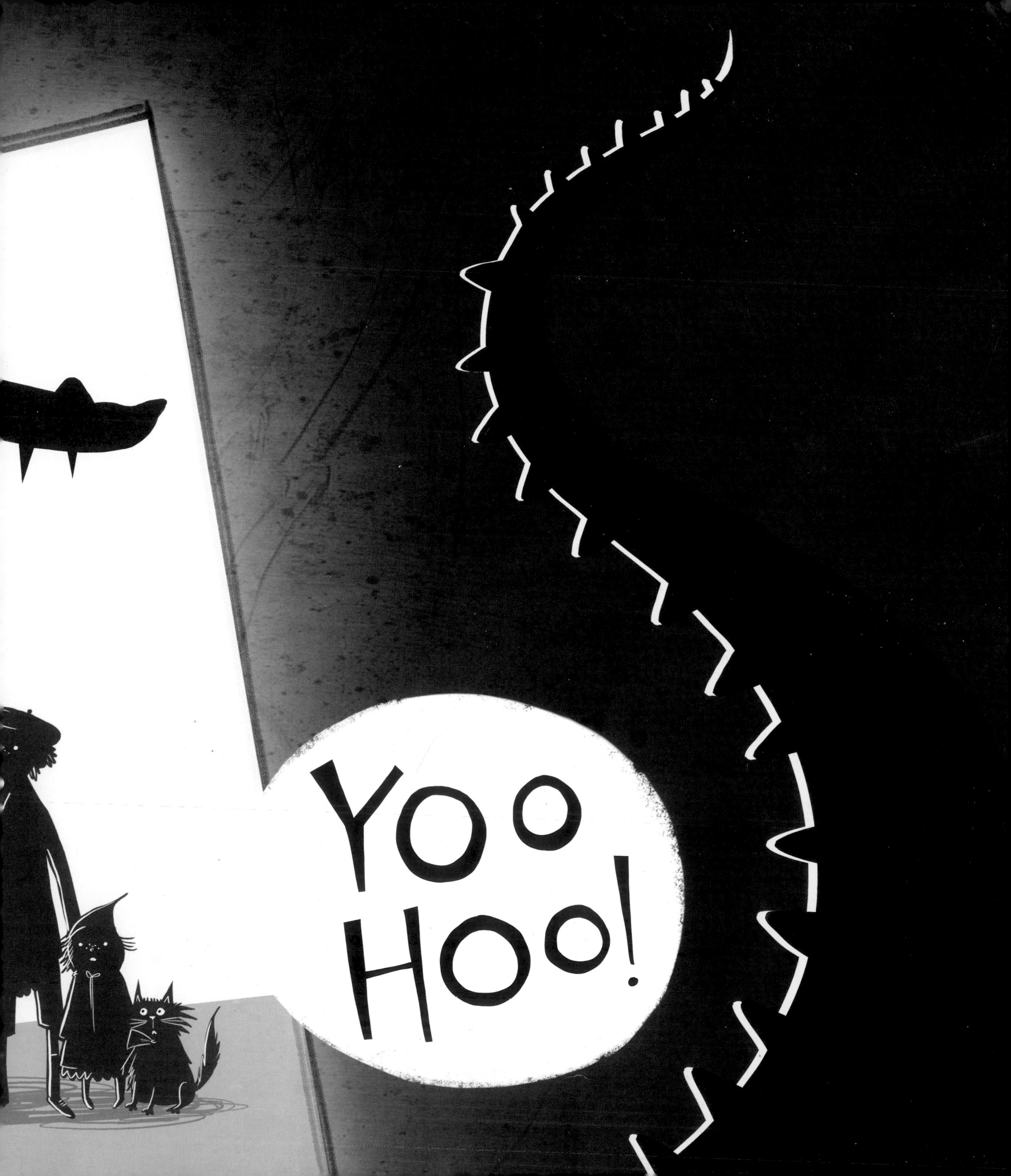
YOO HOO!

And there he stood . . .
their neighbour
(a green and tall-ish chap).
He bowed and said politely,
"Pleased to meet you,
my name's Snap!"

He beckoned to them sweetly,
with a newly sharpened claw,
and said . . .
"Come in my cherry plums.
Don't linger at the door!"

Once ushered in the children
did their best to be polite.
But a crocodile-birthday-boy
was quite a SHOCKING sight!

Snap smiled, "Don't look so worried.
We'll have fun without a doubt.
Now how about a party game?"
Then . . .

RAAAAAAAH!

He
chased
them
all
about!

They ran till they grew tired –
till their little legs grew weak.

Cried Snap,
"I cannot find you!

Are we playing
hide and seek?"

He hunted high and hunted low.
Oh, what a thrilling game!
Then suddenly, he found them –

Boo!

– which was an awful shame . . .

For Snap led them to his table
where there sat one single plate.
And, when the clock struck teatime,
said, "I think it's time I ate!"

He told those dear, sweet children,
"Yes, it's YOU I'm
going to eat.
For nothing could taste nicer –
you're the perfect birthday treat!"

"But, Snap!"
their little voices cried,
"How very wrong you are.
On special days like birthdays
there's a nicer treat by far!"

And suddenly the room went dark,
Snap heard a birthday cheer.

"Hip, hip,

hooray!"

the children cried.

"We've brought you something – here!"

And almost out of thin air,
came a cake all pink and green.
With chocolate drops and candy hearts –

the
BIGGEST
cake you've ever seen!

Snap gulped it down in one great gulp! And –

YUM!

– who would have guessed?
That on special days like birthdays,
children really **don't** taste best!

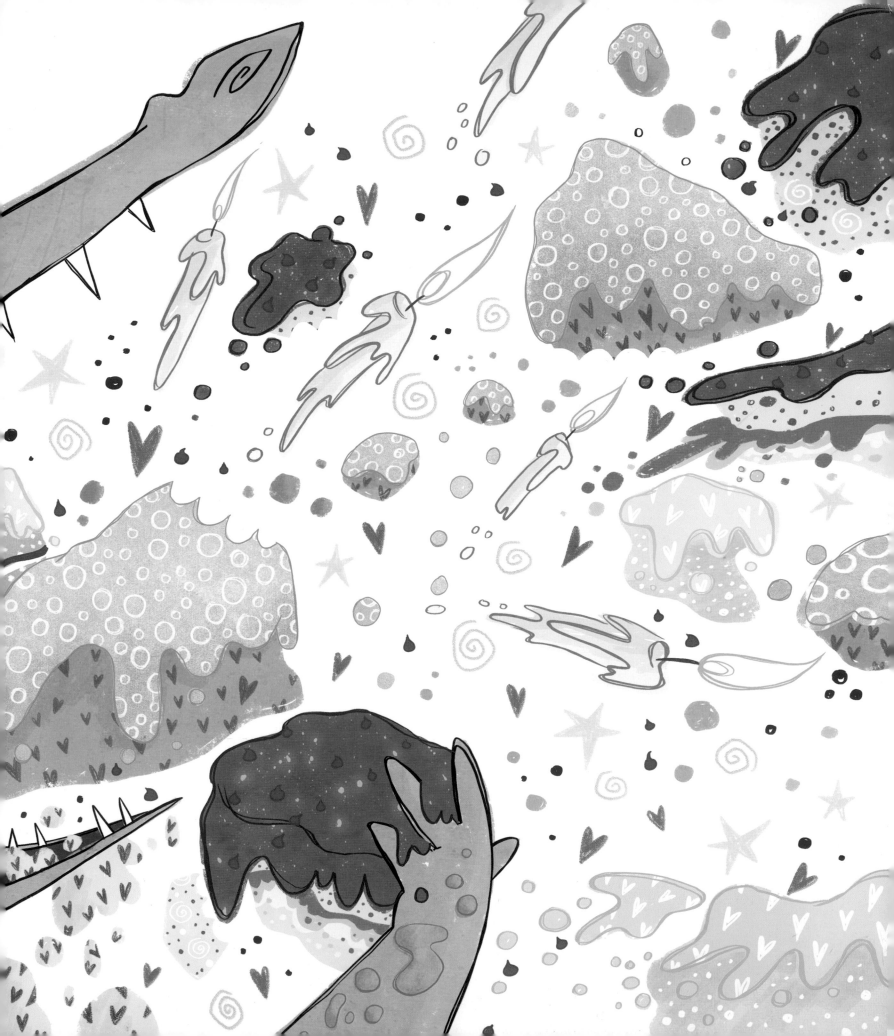

Snap licked his lips and thanked them,
"What a lovely thing to bring!
Yes, it's been fun, now off you run.
I couldn't eat another thing."

For Sarah my Doodle-Muse! – MS

For my Great Grandad Tommy,
who always believed in me and helped me
to achieve my dreams. You will always
have a special place in my heart – LEA

Bloomsbury Publishing, London, New Delhi, New York and Sydney

First Published in Great Britain in 2015 by Bloomsbury Publishing Plc
50 Bedford Square, London, WC1B 3DP

Text copyright © Mark Sperring 2015
Illustrations copyright © Laura Ellen Anderson 2015
The moral rights of the author and illustrator have been asserted

A CIP catalogue record of this book is available from the British Library

ISBN 978 1 4088 5261 3 (HB)
ISBN 978 1 4088 5262 0 (PB)
ISBN 978 1 4088 5260 6 (eBook)

Printed in China by Leo Paper Products, Heshan, Guangdong

1 3 5 7 9 10 8 6 4 2

All papers used by Bloomsbury Publishing are natural, recyclable products made
from wood grown in well-managed forests. The manufacturing processes
conform to the environmental regulations of the country of origin

www.bloomsbury.com

BLOOMSBURY is a registered trademark of Bloomsbury Publishing Plc